Hi, I'm Adrian.

And your name
is...? _ _ _ _ _ _ _ _ _ _ _ _ _ _

It's OK to Be Me!

Just Like You, I Can Do Almost Anything!

Jennifer Moore-Mallinos
Illustrations: Marta Fàbrega

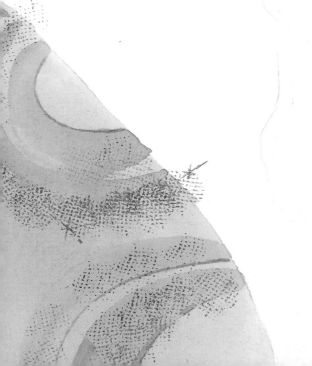

BARRON'S

I'M NEVER ALONE

No matter what I do or where I go, I'm never alone.
I can't go anywhere without it. It comes with me to
school, it's always with me at home, and it even takes
me to the bathroom. I don't know what I would ever
do without my wheelchair!

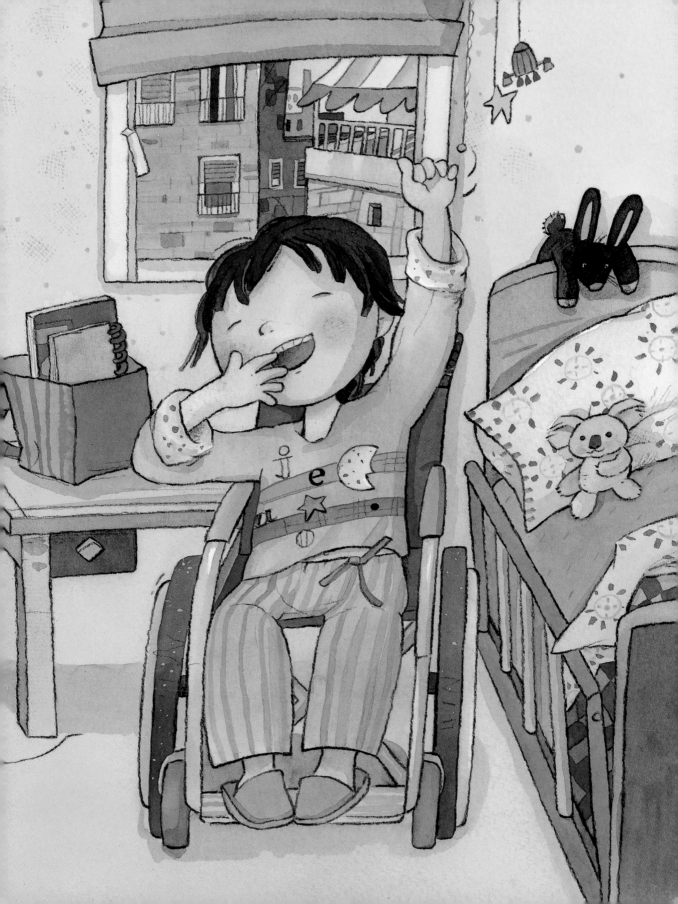

I NEED A WHEELCHAIR

Most people use their legs to get around. Since my
legs don't work well, I need to use a wheelchair.
Wheelchairs come in different sizes and styles.
Some wheelchairs move by a flick of the switch,
whereas others, like mine, move when I push
the wheels forward or backward with my hands,
or when I get pushed by somebody else.

MY WHEELCHAIR IS SPECIAL

I've got an awesome wheelchair, and I designed it all by myself. Blue is my favorite color; so both chair and wheels are bright blue. I even have some cool highlights on my wheels that sparkle when I move. On the back of my chair I have a special pouch to carry my schoolbooks and other stuff. I even have an umbrella that attaches to my chair when it rains.

THE OTHER KIDS

All the kids at school say HI, and everybody loves my sparkly wheels. But they know that I can't participate in any game and so they don't ask me to join them. All I can do is look. Could it be that they're a little scared of me because I move in a wheelchair?

I'M NOT CONTAGIOUS!

Maybe some of the kids think that if they come too close to me they'll catch what I have and their legs will stop working too? Or maybe they're afraid that I won't be able to keep up with them, or that I might get hurt and ruin their game. But I just want to be like everybody else. I just want to have fun.

A GREAT IDEA!

One day after school, while I was
sitting in my wheelchair watching
the neighborhood kids playing
basketball, I had a great idea.
I thought that if I learned how to
use my wheelchair really, really well,
and the kids saw how good I was,
then maybe they would ask me
to play with them.

PRACTICE, PRACTICE, AND MORE PRACTICE!

So that's what I did. I practiced using my wheelchair, all by myself, every day. I practiced so much that I had to start wearing gloves to avoid getting blisters. At first my arm muscles were really sore and tired, but after a while they got bigger and stronger and moving my wheelchair became easier.

STILL PRACTICING!

After I learned how to move my wheelchair forward, backward, and in a circle, I then had to learn how to move through doorways without getting stuck and to turn around furniture and people without bumping into them or running over their toes. I broke a few lamps and squished a lot of toes, but I eventually figured it out! I still get caught in some doorways, once in a while.

THE HARDEST CHALLENGE

Since I couldn't get my wheelchair to go up or down the stairs, it became very important to learn how to use a ramp safely. This was the hardest and scariest thing I had to learn, and there were times when I felt like giving up. But I knew I couldn't, I just had to keep trying!

Going up the ramp without rolling
backwards was tricky and my arms
got very tired, but learning to go down
the ramp slowly was dangerous…
and very scary.
At first it seemed impossible. There
were times when I wanted to give up,
but after lots and lots of practice and
a few close calls I finally figured it out.
All I had to do was take my time.

NOW FOR SOME FUN!

Now that I was really good at getting around in my
wheelchair, it was time to learn how to play basketball.
I already knew the rules of the game just from watching
the neighborhood kids play, but I'd never bounced
a ball or even tried to score a basket before. I guess
it was time for me to learn!

I SHOOT, I SCORE!

I practiced dribbling, first with one hand and then the other. Then Dad set up a bunch of cones for me to move around while I bounced the ball. This was pretty tricky! Throwing the ball through the hoop and scoring a point was the best part, especially when I played a game against Mom and Dad. I didn't always win, but I always had a lot of fun!

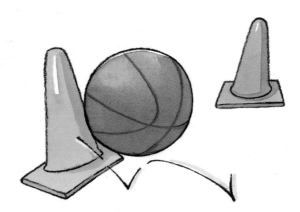